THE MONKEY AND THE CROCODILE

and Other Fables from the Jataka Tales of India

Retold by
ELLEN C. BABBITT

With Illustrations by
ELLSWORTH YOUNG

Dover Publications, Inc.
Mineola, New York

Bibliographical Note

The Monkey and the Crocodile and Other Fables from the Jataka Tales of India, first published by Dover Publications, Inc., in 2015, is a republication of *Jataka Tales,* originally published by The Century Co., New York, in 1918 and *More Jataka Tales,* originally published by The Century Co., New York, in 1922. The original Publisher's Note from *Jataka Tales* is included in the Dover edition.

International Standard Book Number

ISBN-13: 978-0-486-79614-7
ISBN-10: 0-486-79614-0

Manufactured in the United States by Courier Corporation
79614001 2015
www.doverpublications.com

CONTENTS

April 2022

JATAKA TALES

Congratulations &

Thank you!

– Alicia Greenwood

Dedicated

to

DOT

FOREWORD

Long ago I was captivated by the charm of the Jataka Tales and realized the excellent use that might be made of them in the teaching of children. The obvious lessons are many of them suitable for little people, and beneath the obvious there are depths and depths of meaning which they may learn to fathom later on. The Oriental setting lends an additional fascination. I am glad that Miss Babbitt has undertaken to put together this collection, and commend it freely to teachers and parents.

FELIX ADLER.

CONTENTS

PUBLISHER'S NOTE

The Jatakas, or Birth-stories, form one of the sacred books of the Buddhists and relate to the adventures of the Buddha in his former existences, the best character in any story being identified with the Master.

These legends were continually introduced into the religious discourses of the Buddhist teachers to illustrate the doctrines of their faith or to magnify the glory and sanctity of the Buddha, somewhat as medieval preachers in Europe used to enliven their sermons by introducing fables and popular tales to rouse the flagging interest of their hearers.

Sculptured scenes from the Jatakas, found upon the carved railings around the relic shrines of Sanchi and Amaravati and of Bharhut, indicate that the "Birth-stories" were widely known in the third century B.C., and were then considered as part of the sacred history of the religion. At first the tales were probably handed down orally, and it is uncertain when they were put together in systematic form.

ORIGIN OF THE JATAKAS

While some of the stories are Buddhistic and depend for their point on some custom or idea peculiar to Buddhism, many are age-old fables, the flotsam and jetsam of folk-lore, which have appeared under various guises throughout the centuries, as when they were used by Boccaccio or Poggio, merely as merry tales, or by Chaucer, who unwittingly puts a Jataka story into the mouth of his pardoners when he tells the tale of "the Ryotoures three."

Quaint humor and gentle earnestness distinguish these legends and they teach many wholesome lessons, among them the duty of kindness to animals.

Dr. Felix Adler in his "Moral Instruction of Children," says:

> The Jataka Tales contain deep truths, and are calculated to impress lessons of great moral beauty. The tale of the Merchant of Seri, who gave up all that he had in exchange for a golden dish, embodies much the same idea as the parable of the priceless Pearl, in the New Testament. The tale of the Measures of Rice illustrates the importance of a true estimate of values. The tale of the Banyan Deer, which offered its life to save a roe and her young, illustrates self-sacrifice of the noblest sort. The tale of the Sandy Road is one of the finest in the collection.

And he adds that these tales "are, as everyone must admit, nobly conceived, lofty in meaning, and many a helpful sermon might be preached from them as texts."

JATAKA TALES

Jataka Tales

I

THE MONKEY AND THE CROCODILE

PART I

A MONKEY lived in a great tree on a river bank.

In the river there were many Crocodiles. A Crocodile watched the Monkeys for a long time, and one day she said to her son: "My son, get one of those Monkeys for me. I want the heart of a Monkey to eat."

"How am I to catch a Monkey?" asked the little Crocodile. "I do not travel on land, and the Monkey does not go into the water."

"Put your wits to work, and you 'll find a way," said the mother.

And the little Crocodile thought and thought.

At last he said to himself: "I know what I 'll do. I 'll get that Monkey that lives in a big tree on the river bank. He wishes to go across the river to the island where the fruit is so ripe."

So the Crocodile swam to the tree where the Monkey lived. But he was a stupid Crocodile.

"Oh, Monkey," he called, "come with me over to the island where the fruit is so ripe."

"How can I go with you?" asked the Monkey. "I do not swim."

"No—but I do. I will take you over on my back," said the Crocodile.

The Monkey was greedy, and wanted the ripe fruit, so he jumped down on the Crocodile's back.

"Off we go!" said the Crocodile.

"This is a fine ride you are giving me!" said the Monkey.

"Do you think so? Well, how do you like this?" asked the Crocodile, diving.

"Oh, don't!" cried the Monkey, as he went under the water. He was afraid to let go, and he did not know what to do under the water.

When the Crocodile came up, the Monkey sputtered

and choked. "Why did you take me under water, Crocodile?" he asked.

"I am going to kill you by keeping you under water," answered the Crocodile. "My mother wants Monkey-heart to eat, and I 'm going to take yours to her."

"Why did you take me under water, Crocodile?" he asked.

"I wish you had told me you wanted my heart," said the Monkey, "then I might have brought it with me."

"How queer!" said the stupid Crocodile. "Do you mean to say that you left your heart back there in the tree?"

"That is what I mean," said the Monkey. "If you

want my heart, we must go back to the tree and get it. But we are so near the island where the ripe fruit is, please take me there first."

"No, Monkey," said the Crocodile, "I 'll take you straight back to your tree. Never mind the ripe fruit. Get your heart and bring it to me at once. Then we 'll see about going to the island."

"Very well," said the Monkey.

But no sooner had he jumped onto the bank of the river than—whisk! up he ran into the tree.

From the topmost branches he called down to the Crocodile in the water below:

"My heart is way up here! If you want it, come for it, come for it!"

PART II

THE Monkey soon moved away from that tree. He wanted to get away from the Crocodile, so that he might live in peace.

But the Crocodile found him, far down the river, living in another tree.

In the middle of the river was an island covered with fruit-trees.

THE MONKEY AND THE CROCODILE

Half-way between the bank of the river and the island, a large rock rose out of the water. The Monkey could jump to the rock, and then to the island. The Crocodile watched the Monkey crossing from the bank of the river to the rock, and then to the island.

He thought to himself, "The Monkey will stay on the island all day, and I 'll catch him on his way home at night."

The Monkey had a fine feast, while the Crocodile swam about, watching him all day.

Toward night the Crocodile crawled out of the water and lay on the rock, perfectly still.

When it grew dark among the trees, the Monkey started for home. He ran down to the river bank, and there he stopped.

"What is the matter with the rock?" the Monkey thought to himself. "I never saw it so high before. The Crocodile is lying on it!"

But he went to the edge of the water and called: "Hello, Rock!"

No answer.

Then he called again: "Hello, Rock!"

Three times the Monkey called, and then he said:

"Why is it, Friend Rock, that you do not answer me to-night?"

"Oh," said the stupid Crocodile to himself, "the rock answers the Monkey at night. I'll have to answer for the rock this time."

So he answered: "Yes, Monkey! What is it?"

The Monkey laughed, and said: "Oh, it's you, Crocodile, is it?"

"Yes," said the Crocodile. "I am waiting here for you. I am going to eat you."

"You have caught me in a trap this time," said the Monkey. "There is no other way for me to go home. Open your mouth wide so I can jump right into it."

The Monkey jumped.

Now the Monkey well knew that when Crocodiles open their mouths wide, they shut their eyes.

While the Crocodile lay on the rock with his mouth wide open and his eyes shut, the Monkey jumped.

But not into his mouth! Oh, no! He landed on the top of the Crocodile's head, and then sprang quickly to the bank. Up he whisked into his tree.

When the Crocodile saw the trick the Monkey had played on him, he said: "Monkey, you have great cunning. You know no fear. I 'll let you alone after this."

"Thank you, Crocodile, but I shall be on the watch for you just the same," said the Monkey.

II

HOW THE TURTLE SAVED HIS OWN LIFE

A KING once had a lake made in the courtyard for the young princes to play in. They swam about in it, and sailed their boats and rafts on it. One day the king told them he had asked the men to put some fishes into the lake.

Off the boys ran to see the fishes. Now, along with the fishes, there was a Turtle. The boys were delighted with the fishes, but they had never seen a Turtle, and they were afraid of it, thinking it was a demon. They ran back to their father, crying, "There is a demon on the bank of the lake."

The king ordered his men to catch the demon, and to bring it to the palace. When the Turtle was brought in, the boys cried and ran away.

The king was very fond of his sons, so he ordered the men who had brought the Turtle to kill it.

"How shall we kill it?" they asked.

"Pound it to powder," said some one. "Bake it in hot coals," said another.

"Throw the thing into the lake."

So one plan after another was spoken of. Then an old man who had always been afraid of the water said: "Throw the thing into the lake where it flows out over the rocks into the river. Then it will surely be killed."

When the Turtle heard what the old man said, he thrust out his head and asked: "Friend, what have

I done that you should do such a dreadful thing as that to me? The other plans were bad enough, but to throw me into the lake! Don't speak of such a cruel thing!"

When the king heard what the Turtle said, he told his men to take the Turtle at once and throw it into the lake.

The Turtle laughed to himself as he slid away down the river to his old home. "Good!" he said, "those people do not know how safe I am in the water!"

III

THE MERCHANT OF SERI

THERE was once a merchant of Seri who sold brass and tinware. He went from town to town, in company with another man, who also sold brass and tinware. This second man was greedy, getting all he could for nothing, and giving as little as he could for what he bought.

When they went into a town, they divided the streets between them. Each man went up and down the streets he had chosen, calling, "Tinware for sale. Brass for sale." People came out to their door-steps, and bought, or traded, with them.

In one house there lived a poor old woman and her granddaughter. The family had once been rich, but now the only thing they had left of all their riches was a golden bowl. The grandmother did not know it was a golden bowl, but she had kept this because her husband used to eat out of it in the old days. It stood on a shelf among the other pots and pans, and was not often used.

He threw the bowl on the ground.

The greedy merchant passed this house, calling, "Buy my water-jars! Buy my pans!" The granddaughter said: "Oh, Grandmother, do buy something for me!"

"My dear," said the old woman, "we are too poor to buy anything. I have not anything to trade, even."

"Grandmother, see what the merchant will give for the old bowl. We do not use that, and perhaps he will take it and give us something we want for it."

The old woman called the merchant and showed him the bowl, saying, "Will you take this, sir, and give the little girl here something for it?"

The greedy man took the bowl and scratched its side with a needle. Thus he found that it was a golden bowl. He hoped he could get it for nothing, so he said: "What is this worth? Not even a halfpenny." He threw the bowl on the ground, and went away.

By and by the other merchant passed the house. For it was agreed that either merchant might go through any street which the other had left. He called: "Buy my water-jars! Buy my tinware! Buy my brass!"

The little girl heard him, and begged her grandmother to see what he would give for the bowl.

"My child," said the grandmother, "the merchant who was just here threw the bowl on the ground and went away. I have nothing else to offer in trade."

"But, Grandmother," said the girl, "that was a cross man. This one looks pleasant. Ask him. Perhaps he 'll give some little tin dish."

"Call him, then, and show it to him," said the old woman.

As soon as the merchant took the bowl in his hands, he knew it was of gold. He said: "All that I have here is not worth so much as this bowl. It is a golden bowl. I am not rich enough to buy it."

"But, sir, a merchant who passed here a few moments ago, threw it on the ground, saying it was not worth a halfpenny, and he went away," said the grandmother. "It was worth nothing to him. If you value it, take it, giving the little girl some dish she likes for it."

But the merchant would not have it so. He gave the woman all the money he had, and all his wares. "Give me but eight pennies," he said.

So he took the pennies, and left. Going quickly to the river, he paid the boatman the eight pennies to take him across the river.

Soon the greedy merchant went back to the house where he had seen the golden bowl, and said: "Bring that bowl to me, and I will give you something for it."

"No," said the grandmother. "You said the bowl was worthless, but another merchant has paid a great price for it, and taken it away."

"It is a golden bowl."

Then the greedy merchant was angry, crying out, "Through this other man I have lost a small fortune. That bowl was of gold."

He ran down to the riverside, and, seeing the other merchant in the boat out in the river, he called: "Hallo, Boatman! Stop your boat!"

But the man in the boat said: "Don't stop!" So he reached the city on the other side of the river, and lived well for a time on the money the bowl brought him.

IV

THE TURTLE WHO COULD N'T STOP TALKING

A TURTLE lived in a pond at the foot of a hill. Two young wild Geese, looking for food, saw the Turtle, and talked with him. The next day the Geese came again to visit the Turtle and they became very well acquainted. Soon they were great friends.

"Friend Turtle," the Geese said one day, "we have a beautiful home far away. We are going to fly back to it to-morrow It will be a long but pleasant journey. Will you go with us?"

"How could I? I have no wings," said the Turtle.

"Oh, we will take you, if only you can keep your mouth shut, and say not a word to anybody," they said.

"I can do that," said the Turtle. "Do take me with you. I will do exactly as you wish."

So the next day the Geese brought a stick and they held the ends of it. "Now take the middle of this in

"How could I go with you?" said the Turtle.

your mouth, and don't say a word until we reach home," they said.

The Geese sprang into the air.

The Geese then sprang into the air, with the Turtle between them, holding fast to the stick.

The village children saw the two Geese flying along

with the Turtle and cried out: "Oh, see the Turtle up in the air! Look at the Geese carrying a Turtle by a stick! Did you ever see anything more ridiculous in your life!"

The Turtle looked down and began to say, "Well, and if my friends carry me, what business is that of yours?" when he let go, and fell dead at the feet of the children.

As the two Geese flew on, they heard the people say, when they came to see the poor Turtle, "That fellow could not keep his mouth shut. He had to talk, and so lost his life."

"Oh, see the Turtle up in the air."

V

THE OX WHO WON THE FORFEIT

LONG ago a man owned a very strong Ox. The owner was so proud of his Ox, that he boasted to every man he met about how strong his Ox was.

One day the owner went into a village, and said to the men there: "I will pay a forfeit of a thousand pieces of silver if my strong Ox cannot draw a line of one hundred wagons."

The men laughed, and said: "Very well; bring your Ox, and we will tie a hundred wagons in a line and see your Ox draw them along."

So the man brought his Ox into the village. A crowd gathered to see the sight. The hundred carts were in line, and the strong Ox was yoked to the first wagon.

Then the owner whipped his Ox, and said: "Get up, you wretch! Get along, you rascal!"

But the Ox had never been talked to in that way, and he stood still. Neither the blows nor the hard names could make him move.

At last the poor man paid his forfeit, and went sadly

"Get along, you rascal."

home. There he threw himself on his bed and cried: "Why did that strong Ox act so? Many a time he has moved heavier loads easily. Why did he shame me before all those people?"

At last he got up and went about his work. When

he went to feed the Ox that night, the Ox turned to him and said: "Why did you whip me to-day? You never whipped me before. Why did you call me 'wretch' and 'rascal'? You never called me hard names before."

Then the man said: "I will never treat you badly again. I am sorry I whipped you and called you names. I will never do so any more. Forgive me."

"Very well," said the Ox. "To-morrow I will go into the village and draw the one hundred carts for you. You have always been a kind master until to-day. To-morrow you shall gain what you lost."

The next morning the owner fed the Ox well, and hung a garland of flowers about his neck. When they went into the village the men laughed at the man again.

They said: "Did you come back to lose more money?"

"To-day I will pay a forfeit of two thousand pieces of silver if my Ox is not strong enough to pull the one hundred carts," said the owner.

So again the carts were placed in a line, and the Ox was yoked to the first. A crowd came to watch again. The owner said: "Good Ox, show how strong you

A garland of flowers about his neck.

are! You fine, fine creature!" And he patted his neck and stroked his sides.

At once the Ox pulled with all his strength. The carts moved on until the last cart stood where the first had been.

Then the crowd shouted, and they paid back the forfeit the man had lost, saying: "Your Ox is the strongest Ox we ever saw."

And the Ox and the man went home, happy.

VI

THE SANDY ROAD

ONCE upon a time a merchant, with his goods packed in many carts, came to a desert. He was on his way to the country on the other side of the desert.

The sun shone on the fine sand, making it as hot as the top of a stove. No man could walk on it in the sunlight. But at night, after the sun went down, the sand cooled, and then men could travel upon it.

So the merchant waited until after dark, and then set out. Besides the goods that he was going to sell, he took jars of water and of rice, and firewood, so that the rice could be cooked.

All night long he and his men rode on and on. One man was the pilot. He rode first, for he knew the stars, and by them he guided the drivers.

At daybreak they stopped and camped. They unyoked the oxen, and fed them. They built fires and cooked the rice. Then they spread a great awning over all the carts and the oxen, and the men lay down under it to rest until sunset.

They built fires and cooked the rice.

In the early evening, they again built fires and cooked rice. After supper, they folded the awning and put it away. They yoked the oxen, and, as soon as the sand was cool, they started again on their journey across the desert.

Night after night they traveled in this way, resting during the heat of the day. At last one morning the pilot said: "In one more night we shall get out of the sand." The men were glad to hear this, for they were tired.

After supper that night the merchant said: "You may as well throw away nearly all the water and the firewood. By to-morrow we shall be in the city. Yoke the oxen and start on."

Then the pilot took his place at the head of the line. But, instead of sitting up and guiding the drivers, he lay down in the wagon on the cushions. Soon he was fast asleep, because he had not slept for many nights, and the light had been so strong in the daytime that he had not slept well then.

All night long the oxen went on. Near daybreak, the pilot awoke and looked at the last stars fading in the light. "Halt!" he called to the drivers. "We are in the same place where we were yesterday. The oxen must have turned about while I slept."

They unyoked the oxen, but there was no water for them to drink. They had thrown away the water that was left the night before. So the men spread the awning over the carts, and the oxen lay down, tired and thirsty. The men, too, lay down saying, "The wood and water are gone—we are lost."

But the merchant said to himself, "This is no time

for me to sleep. I must find water. The oxen cannot go on if they do not have water to drink. The men must have water. They cannot cook the rice unless they have water. If I give up, we shall all be lost!"

"There must be water somewhere below."

On and on he walked, keeping close watch of the ground. At last he saw a tuft of grass. "There must be water somewhere below, or that grass would not be there," he said.

He ran back, shouting to the men, "Bring the spade and the hammer!"

They jumped up, and ran with him to the spot where the grass grew. They began to dig, and by and by they struck a rock and could dig no further. Then the merchant jumped down into the hole they had dug, and put his ear to the rock. "I hear water running under this rock," he called to them. "We must not give up!" Then the merchant came up out of the hole and said to a serving-lad: "My boy, if you *give* up we are lost! You go down and try!"

The boy stood up straight and raised the hammer high above his head and hit the rock as hard as ever he could. He would not give in. They must be saved. Down came the hammer. This time the rock broke. And the boy had hardly time to get out of the well before it was full of cool water. The men drank as if they never could get enough, and then they watered the oxen, and bathed.

Then they split up their extra yokes and axles, and built a fire, and cooked their rice. Feeling better, they rested through the day. They set up a flag on the well for travelers to see.

At sundown, they started on again, and the next morning reached the city, where they sold the goods, and then returned home.

VII

THE QUARREL OF THE QUAILS

ONCE upon a time many quails lived together in a forest. The wisest of them all was their leader.

A man lived near the forest and earned his living by catching quails and selling them. Day after day he listened to the note of the leader calling the quails. By and by this man, the fowler, was able to call the quails together. Hearing the note the quails thought it was their leader who called.

When they were crowded together, the fowler threw his net over them and off he went into the town, where he soon sold all the quails that he had caught.

The wise leader saw the plan of the fowler for catching the quails. He called the birds to him and said, "This fowler is carrying away so many of us, we must put a stop to it. I have thought of a plan; it is this: The next time the fowler throws a net over you, each of you must put your head through one of the little holes in the net. Then all of you together must fly away to the nearest thorn-bush. You can leave the net on the thorn-bush and be free yourselves."

The quails said that was a very good plan and they would try it the next time the fowler threw the net over them.

The very next day the fowler came and called them together. Then he threw the net over them. The quails lifted the net and flew away with it to the nearest thorn-bush where they left it. They flew back to their leader to tell him how well his plan had worked.

The fowler was busy until evening getting his net off the thorns and he went home empty-handed. The next day the same thing happened, and the next. His wife was angry because he did not bring home any money, but the fowler said, "The fact is those quails are working together now. The moment my net is over them, off they fly with it, leaving it on a thorn-bush. As soon as the quails begin to quarrel I shall be able to catch them."

Not long after this, one of the quails in alighting

on their feeding ground, trod by accident on another's head. "Who trod on my head?" angrily cried the second. "I did; but I didn't mean to. Don't be

The quails lifted the net and flew away with it.

angry," said the first quail, but the second quail was angry and said mean things.

Soon all the quails had taken sides in this quarrel. When the fowler came that day he flung his net over them, and this time instead of flying off with it, one side said, "Now, you lift the net," and the other side said, "Lift it yourself."

"You try to make us lift it all," said the quails on one side. "No, we don't!" said the others, "you begin and we will help," but neither side began.

So the quails quarreled, and while they were quarreling the fowler caught them all in his net. He took them to town and sold them for a good price.

The fowler caught them all in his net.

VIII

THE MEASURE OF RICE

AT one time a dishonest king had a man called the Valuer in his court. The Valuer set the price which ought to be paid for horses and elephants and the other animals. He also set the price on jewelry and gold, and things of that kind.

This man was honest and just, and set the proper price to be paid to the owners of the goods.

The king was not pleased with this Valuer, because he was honest. "If I had another sort of a man as Valuer, I might gain more riches," he thought.

One day the king saw a stupid, miserly peasant come into the palace yard. The king sent for the fellow and asked him if he would like to be the Valuer. The peasant said he would like the position. So the king had him made Valuer. He sent the honest Valuer away from the palace.

Then the peasant began to set the prices on horses

So they went before the king.

and elephants, upon gold and jewels. He did not know their value, so he would say anything he chose. As the king had made him Valuer, the people had to sell their goods for the price he set.

By and by a horse-dealer brought five hundred horses to the court of this king. The Valuer came and said they were worth a mere measure of rice. So the king ordered the horse-dealer to be given the measure of rice, and the horses to be put in the palace stables.

The horse-dealer went then to see the honest man who had been the Valuer, and told him what had happened.

"What shall I do?" asked the horse-dealer.

"I think you can give a present to the Valuer which will make him do and say what you want him to do and say," said the man. "Go to him and give him a fine present, then say to him: 'You said the horses are worth a measure of rice, but now tell what a measure of rice is worth! Can you value that standing in your place by the king?' If he says he can, go with him to the king, and I will be there, too."

The horse-dealer thought this was a good idea. So he took a fine present to the Valuer, and said what the other man had told him to say.

The Valuer took the present, and said: "Yes, I can go before the king with you and tell what a measure of rice is worth. I can value that now."

"Well, let us go at once," said the horse-dealer. So they went before the king and his ministers in the palace.

The horse-dealer bowed down before the king, and said: "O King, I have learned that a measure of rice is the value of my five hundred horses. But will the king be pleased to ask the Valuer what is the value of the measure of rice?"

He ran away from the laughing crowd.

The king, not knowing what had happened, asked: "How now, Valuer, what are five hundred horses worth?"

"A measure of rice, O King!" said he.

"Very good, then! If five hundred horses are worth a measure of rice, what is the measure of rice worth?"

"The measure of rice is worth your whole city," replied the foolish fellow.

The ministers clapped their hands, laughing, and saying, "What a foolish Valuer! How can such a man hold that office? We used to think this great city was beyond price, but this man says it is worth only a measure of rice."

Then the king was ashamed, and drove out the foolish fellow.

"I tried to please the king by setting a low price on the horses, and now see what has happened to me!" said the Valuer, as he ran away from the laughing crowd.

IX

THE FOOLISH, TIMID RABBIT

ONCE upon a time, a Rabbit was asleep under a palm-tree.

All at once he woke up, and thought: "What if the world should break up! What then would become of me?"

At that moment, some Monkeys dropped a cocoanut. It fell down on the ground just back of the Rabbit.

Hearing the noise, the Rabbit said to himself: "The earth is all breaking up!"

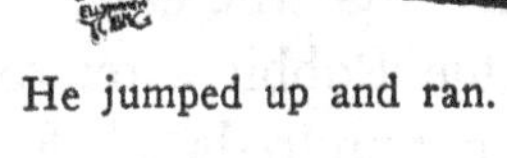

He jumped up and ran.

And he jumped up and ran just as fast as he could, without even looking back to see what made the noise.

Another Rabbit saw him running, and called after him, "What are you running so fast for?"

"Don't ask me!" he cried.

But the other Rabbit ran after him, begging to know what was the matter.

The lion

Then the first Rabbit said: "Don't you know? The earth is all breaking up!"

And on he ran, and the second Rabbit ran with him.

The next Rabbit they met ran with them when he heard that the earth was all breaking up.

One Rabbit after another joined them, until there were hundreds of Rabbits running as fast as they could go.

They passed a Deer, calling out to him that the earth was all breaking up. The Deer then ran with them.

Saw the animals running.

The Deer called to a Fox to come along because the earth was all breaking up.

On and on they ran, and an Elephant joined them.

At last the Lion saw the animals running, and heard their cry that the earth was all breaking up.

He thought there must be some mistake, so he ran to the foot of a hill in front of them and roared three times.

This stopped them, for they knew the voice of the King of Beasts, and they feared him.

"Why are you running so fast?" asked the Lion.

"Oh, King Lion," they answered him, "the earth is all breaking up!"

"Who saw it breaking up?" asked the Lion.

"I did n't," said the Elephant. "Ask the Fox—he told me about it."

"I did n't," said the Fox.

"The Rabbits told me about it," said the Deer.

One after another of the Rabbits said: "I did not see it, but another Rabbit told me about it."

At last the Lion came to the Rabbit who had first said the earth was all breaking up.

"Is it true that the earth is all breaking up?" the Lion asked.

"Yes, O Lion, it is," said the Rabbit. "I was asleep under a palm-tree. I woke up and thought, 'What would become of me if the earth should all break up?' At that very moment, I heard the sound of the earth breaking up, and I ran away."

"Then," said the Lion, "you and I will go back to the place where the earth began to break up, and see what is the matter."

So the Lion put the little Rabbit on his back, and away they went like the wind. The other animals waited for them at the foot of the hill.

The Rabbit told the Lion when they were near the place where he slept, and the Lion saw just where the Rabbit had been sleeping.

He saw, too, the cocoanut that had fallen to the ground near by. Then the Lion said to the Rabbit, "It must have been the sound of the cocoanut falling to the ground that you heard. You foolish Rabbit!"

And the Lion ran back to the other animals, and told them all about it.

If it had not been for the wise King of Beasts, they might be running still.

Away they went like the wind.

X

THE WISE AND THE FOOLISH MERCHANT

ONCE upon a time in a certain country a thrifty merchant visited a great city and bought a great supply of goods. He loaded wagons with the goods, which he was going to sell as he traveled through the country.

A stupid young merchant was buying goods in the same city. He, too, was going to sell what he bought as he traveled through the country.

They were both ready to start at the same time.

The thrifty merchant thought, "We cannot travel together, for the men will find it hard to get wood and water, and there will not be enough grass for so many oxen. Either he or I ought to go first."

So he went to the young man and told him this, saying, "Will you go before or come on after me?"

The other one thought, "It will be better for me to go first. I shall then travel on a road that is not cut up. The oxen will eat grass that has not been touched. The water will be clean. Also, I shall sell my goods at what price I like." So he said, "Friend, I will go on first."

This answer pleased the thrifty merchant. He said to himself, "Those who go before will make the rough places smooth. The old rank grass will have been eaten by the oxen that have gone before, while my oxen will eat the freshly grown tender shoots. Those who go before will dig wells from which we shall drink. Then, too, I will not have to bother about setting prices, but I can sell my goods at the prices set by the other man." So he said aloud, "Very well, friend, you may go on first."

At once the foolish merchant started on his journey. Soon he had left the city and was in the country. By and by he came to a desert which he had to cross. So he filled great water-jars with water, loaded them into a large wagon and started across the desert.

Now on the sands of this desert there lived a wicked demon. This demon saw the foolish young merchant coming and thought to himself, "If I can make him empty those water-jars, soon I shall be able to overcome him and have him in my power."

So the demon went further along the road and changed himself into the likeness of a noble gentleman. He called up a beautiful carriage, drawn by milk-white oxen. Then he called ten other demons, dressed them like men and armed them with bows and arrows, swords and shields. Seated in his carriage, followed by the ten demons, he rode back to meet the merchant. He put mud on the carriage wheels, hung water-lilies and wet grasses upon the oxen and the carriage. Then he made the clothes the demons wore and their hair all wet. Drops of water trickled down over their faces just as if they had all come through a stream.

As the demons neared the foolish merchant they turned their carriage to one side of the way, saying pleasantly, "Where are you going?"

The merchant replied, "We have come from the great city back there and are going across the desert to the villages beyond. You come dripping with mud and carrying water-lilies and grasses. Does it rain on the road you have come by? Did you come through a stream?"

The demon answered, "The dark streak across the sky is a forest. In it there are ponds full of water-

He put mud on the carriage wheels, hung water-lillies and wet grasses upon the oxen and the carriage.

lilies. The rains come often. What have you in all those carts?"

"Goods to be sold," replied the merchant.

"But in that last big heavy wagon what do you carry?" the demon asked.

"Jars full of water for the journey," answered the merchant.

The demon said, "You have done well to bring water as far as this, but there is no need of it beyond. Empty out all that water and go on easily." Then he added, "But we have delayed too long. Drive on!" And he drove on until he was out of sight of the merchant. Then he returned to his home with his followers to wait for the night to come.

The foolish merchant did as the demon bade him and emptied every jar, saving not even a cupful. On and on they traveled and the streak on the sky faded with the sunset. There was no forest, the dark line being only clouds. No water was to be found. The men had no water to drink and no food to eat, for they had no water in which to cook their rice, so they went thirsty and supperless to bed. The oxen, too, were hungry and thirsty and dropped down to sleep here and there. Late at night the demons fell upon them and easily carried off every man. They drove the oxen on ahead of them, but the loaded carts they did not care to take away.

A month and a half after this the wise merchant followed over the same road. He, too, was met on the desert by the demon just as the other had been. But the wise man knew the man was a demon because he cast no shadow. When the demon told him of the ponds in the forest ahead and advised him to throw away the water-jars the wise merchant replied, "We don't throw away the water we have until we get to a place where we see there is more."

Then the demon drove on. But the men who were with the merchant said, "Sir! those men told us that yonder was the beginning of a great forest, and from there onwards it was always raining. Their clothes and hair were dripping with water. Let us throw away the water-jars and go on faster with lighter carts!"

Stopping all the carts the wise merchant asked the men, "Have you ever heard any one say that there was a lake or pond in this desert? You have lived near here always."

"We never heard of a pond or lake," they said.

"Does any man feel a wind laden with dampness blowing against him?" he asked.

"No, sir," they answered.

"Can you see a rain cloud, any of you?" said he.

"No, sir, not one," they said.

"Those fellows were not men, they were demons!" said the wise merchant. "They must have come out to make us throw away the water. Then when we were faint and weak they might have put an end to us. Go on at once and don't throw away a single half-pint of water."

He himself with the head men stood on guard.

So they drove on and before nightfall they came upon the loaded wagons belonging to the foolish merchant.

Then the thrifty merchant had his wagons drawn up in a circle. In the middle of the circle he had the oxen lie down, and also some of the men. He himself with the head men stood on guard, swords in hand and waited for the demons. But the demons did not bother them. Early the next day the thrifty merchant took the best of the wagons left by the foolish merchant and went on safely to the city across the desert.

There he sold all the goods at a profit and returned with his company to his own city.

XI

THE ELEPHANT GIRLY-FACE

ONCE upon a time a king had an Elephant named Girly-face. The Elephant was called Girly-face because he was so gentle and good and looked so kind. "Girly-face never hurts anybody," the keeper of the Elephants often said.

Now one night some robbers came into the courtyard and sat on the ground just outside the stall where Girly-face slept. The talk of the robbers awoke Girly-face.

"This is the way to break into a house," they said. "Once inside the house kill any one who wakens. A robber must not be afraid to kill. A robber must be cruel and have no pity. He must never be good, even for a moment."

Girly-face said to himself, "Those men are teaching me how I should act. I will be cruel. I will show no pity. I will not be good—not even for a moment."

The talk of the robbers awoke Girly-face.

He picked him up in his trunk and threw the poor keeper to the ground.

So the next morning when the keeper came to feed Girly-face he picked him up in his trunk and threw the poor keeper to the ground, killing him.

Another keeper ran to see what the trouble was, and Girly-face killed him, too.

For days and days Girly-face was so ugly that no one dared go near. The food was left for him, but no man would go near him.

By and by the king heard of this and sent one of his wise men to find out what ailed Girly-face.

The wise man had known Girly-face a long time. He looked the Elephant over carefully and could find nothing that seemed to be the matter.

He thought at last, "Girly-face must have heard some bad men talking. Have there been any bad men talking about here?" asked the wise man.

"Yes," one of the keepers said, "a band of robbers were caught here a few weeks ago. They had met in the yard to talk over their plans. They were talking together near the stall where Girly-face sleeps."

So the wise man went back to the king. Said he, "I think Girly-face has been listening to bad talk. If you will send some good men to talk where Girly-

He looked the Elephant over carefully.

face can hear them I think he will be a good Elephant once more."

So that night the king sent a company of the best men to be found to sit and talk near the stall where Girly-face lived. They said to one another, "It is wrong to hurt any one. It is wrong to kill. Every one should be gentle and good."

"Now those men are teaching me," thought Girly-face. "I must be gentle and good. I must hurt no one. I must not kill any one." And from that time on Girly-face was tame and as good as ever an Elephant could be.

XII

THE BANYAN DEER

THERE was once a Deer the color of gold. His eyes were like round jewels, his horns were white as silver, his mouth was red like a flower, his hoofs were bright and hard. He had a large body and a fine tail.

He lived in a forest and was king of a herd of five hundred Banyan Deer. Near by lived another herd of Deer, called the Monkey Deer. They, too, had a king.

The king of that country was fond of hunting the Deer and eating deer meat. He did not like to go alone so he called the people of his town to go with him, day after day.

The townspeople did not like this for while they were gone no one did their work. So they decided to make a park and drive the Deer into it. Then the king could go into the park and hunt and they could go on with their daily work.

They made a park, planted grass in it and provided water for the Deer, built a fence all around it and drove the Deer into it.

Then they shut the gate and went to the king to tell him that in the park near by he could find all the Deer he wanted.

The king went at once to look at the Deer. First he saw there the two Deer kings, and granted them their lives. Then he looked at their great herds.

Some days the king would go to hunt the Deer, sometimes his cook would go. As soon as any of the Deer saw them they would shake with fear and run. But when they had been hit once or twice they would drop down dead.

The King of the Banyan Deer sent for the King of the Monkey Deer and said, "Friend, many of the Deer are being killed. Many are wounded besides those who are killed. After this suppose one from my herd goes up to be killed one day, and the next day let one from your herd go up. Fewer Deer will be lost this way."

The Monkey Deer agreed. Each day the Deer whose turn it was would go and lie down, placing its

The King of the Banyan Deer sent for the King of the Monkey Deer.

head on the block. The cook would come and carry off the one he found lying there.

One day the lot fell to a mother Deer who had a young baby. She went to her king and said, "O King of the Monkey Deer, let the turn pass me by until my baby is old enough to get along without me. Then I will go and put my head on the block."

But the king did not help her. He told her that if the lot had fallen to her she must die.

Then she went to the King of the Banyan Deer and asked him to save her.

"Go back to your herd. I will go in your place," said he.

The next day the cook found the King of the Banyan Deer lying with his head on the block. The cook went to the king, who came himself to find out about this.

"King of the Banyan Deer! did I not grant you your life? Why are you lying here?"

"O great King!" said the King of the Banyan Deer, "a mother came with her young baby and told me that the lot had fallen to her. I could not ask any one else to take her place, so I came myself."

Rise up. I grant your life and hers.

"King of the Banyan Deer! I never saw such kindness and mercy. Rise up. I grant your life and hers. Nor will I hunt any more the Deer in either park or forest."

XIII

THE PRINCES AND THE WATER-SPRITE

ONCE upon a time a king had three sons. The first was called Prince of the Stars. The next was called the Moon Prince and the third was called the Sun Prince. The king was so very happy when the third son was born that he promised to give the queen any boon she might ask.

The queen kept the promise in mind, waiting until the third son was grown before asking the king to give her the boon.

On the twenty-first birthday of the Sun Prince she said to the king, "Great King, when our youngest child was born you said you would give me a boon. Now I ask you to give the kingdom to Sun Prince."

But the king refused, saying that the kingdom must go to the oldest son, for it belonged by right to him. Next it would belong by right to the second son, and not until they were both dead could the kingdom go to the third son.

The queen went away, but the king saw that she was not pleased with his answer. He feared that she would do harm to the older princes to get them out of the way of the Sun Prince.

So he called his elder sons and told them that they must go and live in the forest until his death. "Then come back and reign in the city that is yours by right," he said. And with tears he kissed them on the foreheads and sent them away.

As they were going down out of the palace, after saying good-by to their father, the Sun Prince called to them, "Where are you going?"

And when he heard where they were going and why, he said, "I will go with you, my brothers."

So off they started. They went on and on and by and by they reached the forest. There they sat down to rest in the shade of a pond. Then the eldest brother said to Sun Prince, "Go down to the pond and bathe and drink. Then bring us a drink while we rest here."

Now the King of the Fairies had given this pond to a water-sprite. The Fairy King had said to the water-sprite, "You are to have in your power all who go down into the water except those who give the right answer to one question. Those who give the right answer will not be in your power. The question is, 'What are the Good Fairies like?' "

The Sun Prince went into the pond.

When the Sun Prince went into the pond the water-sprite saw him and asked him the question, "What are the Good Fairies like?"

"They are like the Sun and the Moon," said the Sun Prince.

"You don't know what the Good Fairies are like,"

cried the water-sprite, and he carried the poor boy down into his cave.

By and by the eldest brother said, "Moon Prince, go down and see why our brother stays so long in the pond!"

As soon as the Moon Prince reached the water's edge the water-sprite called to him and said, "Tell me what the Good Fairies are like!"

"Like the sky above us," replied the Moon Prince.

"You don't know, either," said the water-sprite, and dragged the Moon Prince down into the cave where the Sun Prince sat.

"Something must have happened to those two brothers of mine," thought the eldest. So he went to the pond and saw the marks of the footsteps where his brothers had gone down into the water. Then he knew that a water-sprite must live in that pond. He girded on his sword, and stood with his bow in his hand.

The water-sprite soon came along in the form of a woodsman.

"You seem tired, Friend," he said to the prince. "Why don't you bathe in the lake and then lie on the bank and rest?"

The water-sprite in the form of a woodman.

But the prince knew that it was a water-sprite and he said, "You have carried off my brothers!"

"Yes," said the water-sprite.

"Why did you carry them off?"

"Because they did not answer my question," said the water-sprite, "and I have power over all who go down into the water except those who do give the right answer."

"I will answer your question," said the eldest brother. And he did. "The Good Fairies are like

> The pure in heart who fear to sin,
> The good, kindly in word and deed."

"O Wise Prince, I will bring back to you one of your brothers. Which shall I bring?" said the water-sprite.

"Bring me the younger one," said the prince. "It was on his account that our father sent us away. I could never go away with Moon Prince and leave poor Sun Prince here."

"O Wise Prince, you know what the good should do and you are kind. I will bring back both your brothers," said the water-sprite.

After that the three princes lived together in the forest until the king died. Then they went back to the palace. The eldest brother was made king and he had his brothers rule with him. He also built a home for the water-sprite in the palace grounds.

XIV

THE KING'S WHITE ELEPHANT

ONCE upon a time a number of carpenters lived on a river bank near a large forest. Every day the carpenters went in boats to the forest to cut down the trees and make them into lumber.

One day while they were at work an Elephant came limping on three feet to them. He held up one foot and the carpenters saw that it was swollen and sore. Then the Elephant lay down and the men saw that there was a great splinter in the sore foot. They pulled it out and washed the sore carefully so that in a short time it would be well again.

Thankful for the cure, the Elephant thought: "These carpenters have done so much for me, I must be useful to them."

So after that the Elephant used to pull up trees for the carpenters. Sometimes when the trees were chopped down he would roll the logs down to the river.

He held up one foot and the carpenters saw that it was swollen and sore.

Other times he brought their tools for them. And the carpenters used to feed him well morning, noon and night.

Now this Elephant had a son who was white all over—a beautiful, strong young one. Said the old Elephant to himself, "I will take my son to the place in the forest where I go to work each day so that he may learn to help the carpenters, for I am no longer young and strong."

So the old Elephant told his son how the carpenters had taken good care of him when he was badly hurt and took him to them. The white Elephant did

The Elephant used to pull up trees for the carpenters.

as his father told him to do and helped the carpenters and they fed him well.

When the work was done at night the young Elephant went to play in the river. The carpenters' children played with him, in the water and on the bank. He liked to pick them up in his trunk and set them on the high branches of the trees and then let them climb down on his back.

With a last look at his playmates the beautiful white Elephant went on with the king.

THE KING'S WHITE ELEPHANT

One day the king came down the river and saw this beautiful white Elephant working for the carpenters. The king at once wanted the Elephant for his own and paid the carpenters a great price for him. Then with a last look at his playmates, the children, the beautiful white Elephant went on with the king.

The king was proud of his new Elephant and took the best care of him as long as he lived.

XV

THE OX WHO ENVIED THE PIG

ONCE upon a time there was an Ox named Big Red. He had a younger brother named Little Red. These two brothers did all the carting on a large farm.

Now the farmer had an only daughter and she was soon to be married. Her mother gave orders that the Pig should be fattened for the wedding feast.

Little Red noticed that the Pig was fed on choice food. He said to his brother, "How is it, Big Red, that you and I are given only straw and grass to eat, while we do all the hard work on the farm? That lazy Pig does nothing but eat the choice food the farmer gives him."

Said his brother, "My dear Little Red, envy him not. That little Pig is eating the food of death! He is being fattened for the wedding feast. Eat your straw and grass and be content and live long."

Little Red noticed that the Pig was fed on choice food.

The fattened Pig was killed and cooked for the wedding feast.

Not long afterwards the fattened Pig was killed and cooked for the wedding feast.

Then Big Red said, "Did you see, Little Red, what became of the Pig after all his fine feeding?"

"Yes," said the little brother, "we can go on eating plain food for years, but the poor little Pig ate the food of death and now he is dead. His feed was good while it lasted, but it did not last long."

XVI

GRANNY'S BLACKIE

ONCE upon a time a rich man gave a baby Elephant to a woman.

She took the best of care of this great baby and soon became very fond of him.

The children in the village called her Granny, and they called the Elephant "Granny's Blackie."

The Elephant carried the children on his back all over the village. They shared their goodies with him and he played with them.

"Please, Blackie, give us a swing," they said to him almost every day.

"Come on! Who is first?" Blackie answered and picked them up with his trunk, swung them high in the air, and then put them down again, carefully.

But Blackie never did any work.

He ate and slept, played with the children, and visited with Granny.

One day Blackie wanted Granny to go off to the woods with him.

Blackie swung them high in the air.

"I can't go, Blackie, dear. I have too much work to do."

Then Blackie looked at her and saw that she was growing old and feeble.

"I am young and strong," he thought. "I 'll see if I cannot find some work to do. If I could bring some money home to her, she would not have to work so hard."

So next morning, bright and early, he started down to the river bank.

There he found a man who was in great trouble. There was a long line of wagons so heavily loaded that the oxen could not draw them through the shallow water.

When the man saw Blackie standing on the bank he asked, "Who owns this Elephant? I want to hire him to help my Oxen pull these wagons across the river."

A child standing near by said, "That is Granny's Blackie."

"Very well," said the man, "I 'll pay two pieces of silver for each wagon this Elephant draws across the river."

Blackie was glad to hear this promise. He went

into the river, and drew one wagon after another across to the other side.

Then he went up to the man for the money.

The man counted out one piece of silver for each wagon.

When Blackie saw that the man had counted out but one piece of silver for each wagon, instead of two, he would not touch the money at all. He stood in the road and would not let the wagons pass him.

The man tried to get Blackie out of the way, but not one step would he move.

Then the man went back and counted out another piece of silver for each of the wagons and put the silver in a bag tied around Blackie's neck.

Then Blackie started for home, proud to think that he had a present for Granny.

The children had missed Blackie and had asked Granny where he was, but she said she did not know where he had gone.

They all looked for him but it was nearly night before they heard him coming.

"Where have you been, Blackie? And what is that around your neck?" the children cried, running to meet their playmate.

He would not touch the money at all.

Blackie told her that he had earned some money for her.

But Blackie would not stop to talk with his playmates. He ran straight home to Granny.

"Oh, Blackie!" she said, "Where have you been? What is in that bag?" And she took the bag off his neck.

Blackie told her that he had earned some money for her.

"Oh, Blackie, Blackie," said Granny, "how hard you must have worked to earn these pieces of silver! What a good Blackie you are!"

And after that Blackie did all the hard work and Granny rested, and they were both very happy.

XVII

THE CRAB AND THE CRANE

IN the Long Ago there was a summer when very little rain fell.

All the Animals suffered for want of water, but the Fishes suffered most of all.

In one pond full of Fishes, the water was very low indeed.

A Crane sat on the bank watching the Fishes.

"What are you doing?" asked a little Fish.

"I am thinking about you Fishes there in the pond. It is so nearly dry," answered the Crane.

"Yes," the Crane went on, "I was wishing I might do something for you. I know of a pond in the deep woods where there is plenty of water."

"I declare," said the little Fish, "you are the first Crane that ever offered to help a Fish."

"That may be," said the Crane, "but the water is so low in your pond. I could easily carry you one by one on my back to that other pond where there is plenty of water and food and cool shade."

"I don't believe there is any such pond," said the little Fish. "What you wish to do is to eat us, one by one."

"If you don't believe me," said the Crane, "send with me one of the Fishes whom you can believe. I 'll show him the pond and bring him back to tell you all about it."

A big Fish heard the Crane and said, "I will go with you to see the pond—I may as well be eaten by the Crane as to die here."

So the Crane put the big Fish on his back and started for the deep woods.

Soon the Crane showed the big Fish the pool of water. "See how cool and shady it is here," he said, "and how much larger the pond is, and how full it is!"

"Yes!" said the big Fish, "take me back to the little pond and I 'll tell the other Fishes all about it." So back they went.

The Fishes all wanted to go when they heard the big Fish talk about the fine pond which he had seen.

Then the Crane picked up another Fish and car-

So the Crane put the big Fish on his back and started for the deep woods.

ried it away. Not to the pool, but into the woods where the other Fishes could not see them.

Then the Crane put the Fish down and ate it. The Crane went back for another Fish. He carried it to the same place in the woods and ate it, too.

This he did until he had eaten all the Fishes in the pond.

The next day the Crane went to the pond to see if he had left a Fish. There was not one left, but there was a Crab on the sand.

"Little Crab," said the Crane, "would you let me take you to the fine pond in the deep woods where I took the Fishes?"

"But how could you carry me?" asked the Crab.

"Oh, easily," answered the Crane. "I'll take you on my back as I did the Fishes."

"No, I thank you," said the Crab, "I can't go that way. I am afraid you might drop me. If I could take hold of your neck with my claws, I would go. You know we Crabs have a tight grip."

The Crane knew about the tight grip of the Crabs, and he did not like to have the Crab hold on with his claws. But he was hungry, so he said:

"Very well, hold tight."

And off went the Crane with the Crab.

And off went the Crane with the Crab.

When they reached the place where the Crane had eaten the Fishes, the Crane said:

"I think you can walk the rest of the way. Let go of my neck."

"I see no pond," said the Crab. "All I can see is a pile of Fish bones. Is that all that is left of the Fishes?"

"Yes," said the Crane, "and if you will let go of my neck, your shell will be all that will be left of you."

And the Crane put his head down near the ground so that the Crab could get off easily.

But the Crab pinched the Crane's neck so that his head fell off.

"Not my shell, but your bones are left to dry with the bones of the Fishes," said the Crab.

XVIII

WHY THE OWL IS NOT KING OF THE BIRDS

WHY is it that Crows torment the Owls as they sleep in the daytime? For the same reason that the Owls try to kill the Crows while they sleep at night.

Listen to a tale of long ago and then you will see why.

Once upon a time, the people who lived together when the world was young took a certain man for their king. The four-footed animals also took one of their number for their king. The fish in the ocean chose a king to rule over them. Then the birds gathered together on a great flat rock, crying:

"Among men there is a king, and among the beasts, and the fish have one, too; but we birds have none. We ought to have a king. Let us choose one now."

And so the birds talked the matter over and at last they all said, "Let us have the Owl for our king."

"See how sour he looks right now."

No, not all, for one old Crow rose up and said, "For my part, I don't want the Owl to be our king. Look at him now while you are all crying that you want him for your king. See how sour he looks right now. If that's the cross look he wears when he is happy, how will he look when he is angry? I, for one, want no such sour-looking king!"

Then the Crow flew up into the air crying, "I don't

like it! I don't like it!" The Owl rose and followed him. From that time on the Crows and the Owls have been enemies. The birds chose a Turtle Dove to be their king, and then flew to their homes.

MORE JATAKA TALES

DEDICATED

to

RUDYARD KIPLING

in the name of all children
who troop to his call

FOREWORD

The continued success of the "Jataka Tales," as retold and published ten years ago, has led to this second and companion volume. Who that has read or told stories to children has not been lured on by the subtle flattery of their cry for "more"?

Dr. Felix Adler, in his Foreword to "Jataka Tales," says that long ago he was "captivated by the charm of the Jataka Tales." Little children have not only felt this charm, but they have discovered that they can read the stories to themselves. And so "More Jataka Tales" were found in the volume translated from the Sanskrit into English by a group of Cambridge scholars and published by the University Press.

The Jataka tales, regarded as historic in the Third Century B. C., are the oldest collection of folk-lore extant. They come down to us from that dim for-off time when our forebears told tales around the same hearthfire on the roof of the world. Professor Rhys Davids speaks of them as "a priceless record of the childhood of our race. The same stories are found in Greek, Latin, Arabic, Persian, and in most European languages. The Greek versions of the Jataka tales were adapted and ascribed to the famous story-teller, Æsop, and under his name handed down as a continual feast for the children in the West,—tales first invented to please and instruct our far-off cousins in the East." Here East, though East, meets West!

A "Guild of Jataka Translators," under Professor E. B. Cowell, professor of Sanskrit in the University of Cambridge, brought out the complete edition of the Jataka between 1895 and 1907. It is from this source that "Jataka Tales" and "More Jataka Tales" have been retold.

Of these stories, spread over Europe through literary channels, Professor Cowell says, "They are the stray waifs of literature, in the course of their long wanderings coming to be recognized under widely different aspects, as when they are used by Boccaccio, or Chaucer, or La Fontaine."

CONTENTS

CONTENTS

MORE JATAKA TALES

MORE JATAKA TALES

I

THE GIRL MONKEY AND THE STRING OF PEARLS

ONE day the king went for a long walk in the woods. When he came back to his own garden, he sent for his family to come down to the lake for a swim.

When they were all ready to go into the water, the queen and her ladies left their jewels in charge of the servants, and then went down into the lake.

As the queen put her string of pearls away in a box, she was watched by a Girl Monkey who sat in the branches of a tree near-by. This Girl Monkey wanted to get the queen's string of pearls, so she sat still and watched, hoping that the servant in charge of the pearls would go to sleep.

At first the servant kept her eyes on the jewel-box. But by and by she began to nod, and then she fell fast asleep.

As soon as the Monkey saw this, quick as the wind she jumped down, opened the box, picked up the string of pearls, and quick as the wind she was up in the tree again, holding the pearls very carefully. She put the string of pearls on, and then, for fear the guards in the garden would see the pearls, the Monkey hid them in a hole in the tree. Then she sat near-by looking as if nothing had happened.

By and by the servant awoke. She looked in the box, and finding that the string of pearls was not there, she cried, "A man has run off with the queen's string of pearls."

Up ran the guards from every side.

The servant said: "I sat right here beside the box where the queen put her string of pearls. I did not move from the place. But the day is hot, and I was tired. I must have fallen asleep. The pearls were gone when I awoke."

The guards told the king that the pearls were gone.

"Find the man who stole the pearls," said the king. Away went the guards looking high and low for the thief.

After the king had gone, the chief guard said to himself:

"There is something strange here. These pearls," thought he, "were lost in the garden. There was a strong guard at the gates, so that no one from the outside could get into the garden. On the other hand, there are hundreds of

Monkeys here in the garden. Perhaps one of the Girl Monkeys took the string of pearls."

Then the chief guard thought of a trick that would tell whether a Girl Monkey had taken the pearls. So he bought a number of strings of bright-colored glass beads.

After dark that night the guards hung the strings of glass beads here and there on the low bushes in the garden. When the Monkeys saw the strings of bright-colored beads the next morning, each Monkey ran for a string.

But the Girl Monkey who had taken the queen's string of pearls did not come down. She sat near the hole where she had hidden the pearls.

The other Monkeys were greatly pleased with their strings of beads. They chattered to one another about them. "It is too bad you did not get one," they said to her as she sat quietly, saying nothing. At last she could stand it no longer. She put on the queen's string of pearls and came down, saying proudly: "You have only strings of glass beads. See my string of pearls!"

Then the chief of the guards, who had been hiding near-by, caught the Girl Monkey. He took her at once to the king.

"It was this Girl Monkey, your Majesty, who took the pearls."

The king was glad enough to get the pearls, but he asked the chief guard how he had found out who took them.

The chief guard told the king that he knew no one could have come into the garden and so he thought they must have been taken by one of the Monkeys in the garden. Then he told the king about the trick he had played with the beads.

"You are the right man in the right place," said the king, and he thanked the chief of the guards over and over again.

II

THE THREE FISHES

ONCE upon a time three Fishes lived in a far-away river. They were named Thoughtful, Very-Thoughtful, and Thoughtless.

One day they left the wild country where no men lived, and came down the river to live near a town.

Very-Thoughtful said to the other two: "There is danger all about us here. Fishermen come to the river here to catch fish with all sorts of nets and lines. Let us go back again to the wild country where we used to live."

But the other two Fishes were so lazy and so greedy that they kept putting off their going from day to day.

But one day Thoughtful and Thoughtless went swimming on ahead of Very-Thoughtful and they did not see the fisherman's net and rushed into it. Very-Thoughtful saw them rush into the net.

"I must save them," said Very-Thoughtful.

So swimming around the net, he splashed in the water in

front of it, like a Fish that had broken through the net and gone up the river. Then he swam back of the net and

splashed about there like a Fish that had broken through and gone down the river.

The fisherman saw the splashing water and thought the Fishes had broken through the net and that one had gone up the river, the other down, so he pulled in the net by one corner. That let the two Fishes out of the net and away they went to find Very-Thoughful.

"You saved our lives, Very-Thoughtful," they said, "and now we are willing to go back to the wild country."

So back they all went to their old home where they lived safely ever after.

III

THE TRICKY WOLF AND THE RATS

ONCE upon a time a Big Rat lived in the forest, and many hundreds of other Rats called him their Chief.

A Tricky Wolf saw this troop of Rats, and began to plan how he could catch them. He wanted to eat them, but how was he to get them? At last he thought of a plan. He went to a corner near the home of the Rats and waited until he saw one of them coming. Then he stood up on his hind legs.

The Chief of the Rats said to the Wolf, "Wolf, why do you stand on your hind legs?"

"Because I am lame," said the Tricky Wolf. "It hurts me to stand on my front legs."

"And why do you keep your mouth open?" asked the Rat.

"I keep my mouth open so that I may drink in all the air I can," said the Wolf. "I live on air; it is my only food day after day. I can not run or walk, so I stay here. I

try not to complain." When the Rats went away the Wolf lay down.

The Chief of the Rats was sorry for the Wolf, and he went each night and morning with all the other Rats to talk with the Wolf, who seemed so poor, and who did not complain.

Each time as the Rats were leaving, the Wolf caught and ate the last one. Then he wiped his lips, and looked as if nothing had happened.

Each night there were fewer Rats at bedtime. Then they asked the Chief of the Rats what the trouble was. He could not be sure, but he thought the Wolf was to blame.

So the next day the Chief said to the other Rats, "You go first this time and I will go last."

They did so, and as the Chief of the Rats went by, the

Wolf made a spring at him. But the Wolf was not quick enough, and the Chief of the Rats got away.

"So this is the food you eat. Your legs are not so lame as they were. You have played your last trick, Wolf," said the Chief of the Rats, springing at the Wolf's throat. He bit the Wolf, so that he died.

And ever after the Rats lived happily in peace and quiet.

IV

THE WOODPECKER, TURTLE, AND DEER

ONCE upon a time a Deer lived in a forest near a lake. Not far from the same lake, a Woodpecker had a nest in the top of a tree; and in the lake lived a Turtle. The three were friends, and lived together happily.

A hunter, wandering about in the wood, saw the footprints of the Deer near the edge of the lake. "I must trap the Deer, going down into the water," he said, and setting a strong trap of leather, he went his way.

Early that night when the Deer went down to drink, he was caught in the trap, and he cried the cry of capture.

At once the Woodpecker flew down from her tree-top, and the Turtle came out of the water to see what could be done.

Said the Woodpecker to the Turtle: "Friend, you have teeth; you gnaw through the leather trap. I will go and see to it that the hunter keeps away. If we both do our best our friend will not lose his life."

So the Turtle began to gnaw the leather, and the Woodpecker flew to the hunter's house.

At dawn the hunter came, knife in hand, to the front door

of his house.

The Woodpecker, flapping her wings, flew at the hunter and struck him in the face.

The hunter turned back into the house and lay down for a little while. Then he rose up again, and took his knife. He said to himself: "When I went out by the front door, a Bird flew in my face; now I will go out by the back door." So he did.

The Woodpecker thought: "The hunter went out by the front door before, so now he will leave by the back door." So the Woodpecker sat in a tree near the back door.

When the hunter came out the bird flew at him again, flapping her wings in the hunter's face.

Then the hunter turned back and lay down again. When the sun arose, he took his knife, and started out once more.

This time the Woodpecker flew back as fast as she could fly to her friends, crying, "Here comes the hunter!"

By this time the Turtle had gnawed through all the pieces of the trap but one. The leather was so hard that it made his teeth feel as if they would fall out. His mouth was all covered with blood. The Deer heard the Woodpecker, and saw the hunter, knife in hand, coming on. With a strong pull the Deer broke this last piece of the trap, and ran into the woods.

The Woodpecker flew up to her nest in the tree-top.

But the Turtle was so weak he could not get away. He

lay where he was. The hunter picked him up and threw him into a bag, tying it to a tree.

The Deer saw that the Turtle was taken, and made up his mind to save his friend's life. So the Deer let the hunter see him.

The hunter seized his knife and started after the Deer. The Deer, keeping just out of his reach, led the hunter into the forest.

When the Deer saw that they had gone far into the forest he slipped away from the hunter, and swift as the wind, he went by another way to where he had left the Turtle.

But the Turtle was not there. The Deer called, "Turtle, Turtle!"; and the Turtle called out, "Here I am in a bag hanging on this tree."

Then the Deer lifted the bag with his horns, and throwing it upon the ground, he tore the bag open, and let the Turtle out.

The Woodpecker flew down from her nest, and the Deer said to them: "You two friends saved my life, but if we stay here talking, the hunter will find us, and we may not get away. So do you, Friend Woodpecker, fly away. And you, Friend Turtle, dive into the water. I will hide in the forest."

The hunter did come back, but neither the Deer, nor the Turtle, nor the Woodpecker was to be seen. He found his torn bag, and picking that up he went back to his home.

The three friends lived together all the rest of their lives.

V

THE GOLDEN GOOSE

ONCE upon a time there was a Goose who had beautiful golden feathers. Not far away from this Goose lived a poor, a very poor woman, who had two daughters. The Goose saw that they had a hard time to get along and said he to himself:

"If I give them one after another of my golden feathers, the mother can sell them, and with the money they bring she and her daughters can then live in comfort."

So away the Goose flew to the poor woman's house.

Seeing the Goose, the woman said: "Why do you come here? We have nothing to give you."

"But I have something to give you," said the Goose. "I will give my feathers, one by one, and you can sell them for enough so that you and your daughters can live in comfort."

So saying the Goose gave her one of his feathers, and then flew away. From time to time he came back, each time leaving another feather.

The mother and her daughters sold the beautiful feathers for enough money to keep them in comfort. But one day the mother said to her daughters: "Let us not trust this Goose. Some day he may fly away and never come back.

Then we should be poor again. Let us get all of his feathers the very next time he comes."

The daughters said: "This will hurt the Goose. We will not do such a thing."

But the mother was greedy. The next time the Golden

Goose came she took hold of him with both hands, and pulled out every one of his feathers.

Now the Golden Goose has strange feathers. If his feathers are plucked out against his wish, they no longer re-

main golden but turn white and are of no more value than chicken-feathers. The new ones that come in are not golden, but plain white.

As time went on his feathers grew again, and then he flew away to his home and never came back again.

VI

THE STUPID MONKEYS

ONCE upon a time a king gave a holiday to all the people in one of his cities.

The king's gardener thought to himself: "All my friends are having a holiday in the city. I could go into the city and enjoy myself with them if I did not have to water the trees here in this garden. I know what I will do. I will get the Monkeys to water the young trees for me." In those days, a tribe of Monkeys lived in the king's garden.

So the gardener went to the Chief of the Monkeys, and said: "You are lucky Monkeys to be living in the king's garden. You have a fine place to play in. You have the best of food—nuts, fruit, and the young shoots of trees to eat. You have no work at all to do. You can play all day, every day. To-day my friends are having a holiday in the city, and I want to enjoy myself with them. Will you water the young trees so that I can go away?"

"Oh, yes!" said the Chief of the Monkeys. "We shall be glad to do that."

"Do not forget to water the trees when the sun goes down. See they have plenty of water, but not too much," said the gardener. Then he showed them where the watering-pots were kept, and went away.

When the sun went down the Monkeys took the watering-pots, and began to water the young trees. "See that each tree has enough water," said the Chief of the Monkeys.

"How shall we know when each tree has enough?" they asked. The Chief of the Monkeys had no good answer, so he said: "Pull up each young tree and look at the length of its roots. Give a great deal of water to those with long roots, but only a little to those trees that have short roots."

Then those stupid Monkeys pulled up all the young trees to see which trees had long roots and which had short roots.

When the gardener came back the next day, the poor young trees were all dead.

VII

THE CUNNING WOLF

ONCE upon a time the people in a certain town went out into the woods for a holiday. They took baskets full of good things to eat. But when noontime came they ate all the meat they had brought with them, not leaving any for supper.

"I will get some fresh meat. We will make a fire here and roast it," said one of the men.

So taking a club, he went to the lake where the animals came to drink. He lay down, club in hand, pretending to be dead.

When the animals came down to the lake they saw the man lying there and they watched him for some time.

"That man is playing a trick on us, I believe," said the King of the Wolves. "The rest of you stay here while I will see whether he is really dead, or whether he is pretending to be dead."

Then the cunning King of the Wolves crept up to the man and slyly pulled at his club.

At once the man pulled back on his club.

Then the King of the Wolves ran off saying: "If you had been dead, you would not have pulled back on your club when I tried to pull it away. I see your trick. You pre-

tend you are dead so that you may kill one of us for your supper."

The man jumped up and threw his club at the King of the Wolves. But he missed his aim. He looked for the other animals but there was not one in sight. They had all run away.

Then the man went back to his friends, saying: "I tried to get fresh meat by playing a trick on the animals, but the cunning Wolf played a better trick on me, and I could not get one of them."

VIII

THE PENNY-WISE MONKEY

ONCE upon a time the king of a large and rich country gathered together his army to take a far-away little country.

The king and his soldiers marched all morning long and then went into camp in the forest.

When they fed the horses they gave them some peas to eat. One of the Monkeys living in the forest saw the peas and jumped down to get some of them. He filled his mouth and hands with them, and up into the tree he went again, and sat down to eat the peas.

As he sat there eating the peas, one pea fell from his hand to the ground. At once the greedy Monkey dropped all the peas he had in his hands, and ran down to hunt for the lost pea. But he could not find that one pea. He climbed up into his tree again, and sat still looking very glum. "To get more, I threw away what I had," he said to himself.

The king had watched the Monkey, and he said to him-

self: "I will not be like this foolish Monkey, who lost much to gain a little. I will go back to my own country and enjoy what I now have."

So he and his men marched back home.

IX

THE RED-BUD TREE

ONCE upon a time four young princes heard a story about a certain wonderful tree, called the Red-Bud Tree. No one of them had ever seen a Red-Bud Tree, and each prince wished to be the first to see one.

So the eldest prince asked the driver of the king's chariot to take him deep into the woods where this tree grew. It was still very early in the spring and the tree had no leaves, nor buds. It was black and bare like a dead tree. The prince could not understand why this was called a Red-Bud Tree, but he asked no questions.

Later in the spring, the next son went with the driver of the king's chariot to see the Red-Bud Tree. At this time it was covered with red buds.

The tree was all covered with green leaves when the third son went into the woods a little later to see it. He asked no questions about it, but he could see no reason for calling it the Red-Bud Tree.

Some time after this the youngest prince begged to be

taken to see the Red-Bud Tree. By this time it was covered with little bean-pods.

When he came back from the woods he ran into the garden where his brothers were playing, crying, "I have seen the Red-Bud Tree."

"So have I," said the eldest prince. "It did not look like much of a tree to me," said he; "it looked like a dead tree. It was black and bare."

"What makes you say that?" said the second son. "The tree has hundreds of beautiful red buds. This is why it is called the Red-Bud Tree."

The third prince said: "Red buds, did you say? Why do you say it has red buds? It is covered with green leaves."

The prince who had seen the tree last laughed at his brothers, saying: "I have just seen that tree, and it is not like a dead tree. It has neither red buds nor green leaves on it. It is covered with little bean-pods."

The king heard them and waited until they stopped talking. Then he said: "My sons, you have all four seen the same tree, but each of you saw it at a different time of the year."

X

THE WOODPECKER AND THE LION

ONE day while a Lion was eating his dinner a bone stuck in his throat. It hurt so that he could not finish his dinner. He walked up and down, up and down, roaring with pain.

A Woodpecker lit on a branch of a tree near-by, and hearing the Lion, she said, "Friend, what ails you?" The Lion told the Woodpecker what the matter was, and the Woodpecker said: "I would take the bone out of your throat, friend, but I do not dare to put my head into your mouth, for fear I might never get it out again. I am afraid you might eat me."

"O Woodpecker, do not be afraid," the Lion said. "I will not eat you. Save my life if you can!"

"I will see what I can do for you," said the Woodpecker. "Open your mouth wide." The Lion did as he was told, but the Woodpecker said to himself: "Who knows what this Lion will do? I think I will be careful."

So the Woodpecker put a stick between the Lion's upper and lower jaws so that he could not shut his mouth.

Then the Woodpecker hopped into the Lion's mouth and hit the end of the bone with his beak. The second time he hit it, the bone fell out.

The Woodpecker hopped out of the Lion's mouth, and hit the stick so that it too fell out. Then the Lion could shut his mouth.

At once the Lion felt very much better, but not one word of thanks did he say to the Woodpecker.

One day later in the summer, the Woodpecker said to the Lion, "I want you to do something for me."

"Do something for you?" said the Lion. "You mean you want me to do something more for you. I have already done a great deal for you. You cannot expect me to do anything more for you. Do not forget that once I had you in my mouth, and I let you go. That is all that you can ever expect me to do for you."

The Woodpecker said no more, but he kept away from the Lion from that day on.

XI

THE OTTERS AND THE WOLF

ONE day a Wolf said to her mate, "A longing has come upon me to eat fresh fish."

"I will go and get some for you," said he and he went down to the river.

There he saw two Otters standing on the bank looking for fish. Soon one of the Otters saw a great fish, and entering the water with a bound, he caught hold of the tail of the fish.

But the fish was strong and swam away, dragging the Otter after him. "Come and help me," the Otter called back to his friend. "This great fish will be enough for both of us!"

So the other Otter went into the water. The two together were able to bring the fish to land. "Let us divide the fish into two parts."

"I want the half with the head on," said one.

"You cannot have that half. That is mine," said the other. "You take the tail."

The Wolf heard the Otters and he went up to them.

Seeing the Wolf, the Otters said: "Lord of the gray-grass color, this fish was caught by both of us together. We cannot agree about dividing him. Will you divide him for us?"

The Wolf cut off the tail and gave it to one, giving the head to the other. He took the large middle part for him-

self, saying to them, "You can eat the head and the tail without quarreling." And away he ran with the body of the fish. The Otters stood and looked at each other. They had nothing to say, but each thought to himself that the Wolf had run off with the best of the fish.

The Wolf was pleased and said to himself, as he ran toward home, "Now I have fresh fish for my mate."

His mate, seeing him coming, came to meet him, saying: "How did you get fish? You live on land, not in the water."

Then he told her of the quarrel of the Otters. "I took the fish as pay for settling their quarrel," said he.

XII

HOW THE MONKEY SAVED HIS TROOP

A MANGO-TREE grew on the bank of a great river. The fruit fell from some of the branches of this tree into the river, and from other branches it fell on the ground.

Every night a troop of Monkeys gathered the fruit that lay on the ground and climbed up into the tree to get the mangoes, which were like large, juicy peaches.

One day the king of the country stood on the bank of this same river, but many miles below where the mango-tree grew. The king was watching the fishermen with their nets.

As they drew in their nets, the fishermen found not only fishes but a strange fruit. They went to the king with the strange fruit. "What is this?" asked the king.

"We do not know, O King," they said.

"Call the foresters," said the king, "They will know what it is."

So they called the foresters and they said that it was a mango.

"Is it good to eat?" asked the king.

The foresters said it was very good. So the king cut the

mango and giving some to the princes, he ate some of it himself. He liked it very much, and they all liked it.

Then the king said to the foresters, "Where does the mango-tree grow?"

The foresters told him that it grew on the river bank many miles farther up the river.

"Let us go and see the tree and get some mangoes," said the king.

So he had many rafts joined together, and they went up the river until they came to the place where the mango-tree grew.

The foresters said, "O King, this is the mango-tree."

"We will land here," said the king, and they did so. The king and all the men with him gathered the mangoes that lay on the ground under the tree. They all liked them so well that the king said, "Let us stay here to-night, and gather more fruit in the morning." So they had their supper under the trees, and then lay down to sleep.

When all was quiet, the Chief of the Monkeys came with his troop. All the mangoes on the ground had been eaten, so the monkeys jumped from branch to branch, picking and eating mangoes, and chattering to one another. They made so much noise that they woke up the king. He called his archers saying: "Stand under the mango-tree and shoot the Monkeys as they come down to the ground to get away. Then in the morning we shall have Monkey's flesh as well as mangoes to eat."

The Monkeys saw the archers standing around with their

arrows ready to shoot. Fearing death, the Monkeys ran to their Chief, saying: "O Chief, the archers stand around the tree ready to shoot us! What shall we do?" They shook with fear.

The Chief said: "Do not fear; I will save you. Stay where you are until I call you."

The Monkeys were comforted, for he had always helped them whenever they had needed help.

Then the Chief of the Monkeys ran out on the branch of the mango-tree that hung out over the river. The long branches of the tree across the river did not quite meet the branch he stood on. The Chief said to himself: "If the Monkeys try to jump across from this tree to that, some of them will fall into the water and drown. I must save them, but how am I to do it? I know what I shall do. I shall make a bridge of my back."

So the Chief reached across and took hold of the longest branch of the tree across the river. He called, "Come, Monkeys; run out on this branch, step on my back, and then run along the branch of the other tree."

The Monkeys did as the Chief told them to do. They ran along the branch, stepped on his back, then ran along the branch of the other tree. They swung themselves down to the ground, and away they went back to their home.

The king saw all that was done by the Chief and his troop. "That big Monkey," said the king to the archers, "saved the whole troop. I will see to it that he is taken care of the rest of his life."

And the king kept his promise.

XIII

THE HAWKS AND THEIR FRIENDS

A FAMILY of Hawks lived on an island in a lake not far from the great forest. On the northern shore of this lake lived a Lion, King of Beasts. On the eastern shore lived a Kingfisher. On the southern shore of the lake lived a Turtle.

"Have you many friends near here?" the Mother Hawk asked the Father Hawk.

"No, not one in this part of the forest," he said.

"You must find some friends. We must have some one who can help us if ever we are in danger, or in trouble," said the Mother Hawk.

"With whom shall I make friends?" asked the Father Hawk.

"With the Kingfisher, who lives on the eastern shore, and with the Lion on the north," said the Mother Hawk, "and with the Turtle who lives on the southern shore of this lake."

The Father Hawk did so.

THE HAWKS AND THEIR FRIENDS

One day men hunted in the great forest from morning until night, but found nothing. Not wishing to go home empty-handed, they went to the island to see what they could find there.

"Let us stay here to-night," they said, "and see what we can find in the morning."

So they made beds of leaves for themselves and lay down to sleep. They had made their beds under the tree in which the Hawks had their nest.

But the hunters could not go to sleep because they were bothered by the flies and mosquitoes. At last the hunters got up and made a fire on the shore of the lake, so that the smoke would drive away the flies and mosquitoes. The smoke awoke the birds, and the young ones cried out.

"Did you hear that?" said one of the hunters. "That was the cry of birds! They will do very well for our breakfast. There are young ones in that nest." And the hunters put more wood on the fire, and made it blaze up.

Then the Mother bird said to the Father: "These men are planning to eat our young ones. We must ask our friends to save us. Go to the Kingfisher and tell him what danger we are in."

The Father Hawk flew with all speed to the Kingfisher's nest and woke him with his cry.

"Why have you come?" asked the Kingfisher.

Then the Father Hawk told the Kingfisher what the hunters planned to do.

"Fear not," said the Kingfisher. "I will help you. Go back quickly and comfort my friend your mate, and say that I am coming."

So the Father Hawk flew back to his nest, and the Kingfisher flew to the island and went into the lake near the place where the fire was burning.

While the Father Hawk was away, one of the hunters had climbed up into the tree. Just as he neared the nest, the Kingfisher, beating the water with his wings, sprinkled water on the fire and put it out.

Down came the hunter to make another fire. When it was burning well he climbed the tree again. Once more the Kingfisher put it out. As often as a fire was made, the Kingfisher put it out. Midnight came and the Kingfisher was now very tired.

The Mother Hawk noticed this and said to her mate: "The Kingfisher is tired out. Go and ask the Turtle to help us so that the Kingfisher may have a rest."

The Father Hawk flew down and said, "Rest awhile, Friend Kingfisher; I will go and get the Turtle."

So the Father Hawk flew to the southern shore and wakened the Turtle.

"What is your errand, Friend?" asked the Turtle.

"Danger has come to us," said the Father Hawk, and he told the Turtle about the hunters. "The Kingfisher has been working for hours, and now he is very tired. That is why I have come to you."

The Turtle said, "I will help you at once."

Then the Turtle went to the island where the Hawks lived. He dived into the water, collected some mud, and put out the fire with it. Then he lay still.

The hunters cried: "Why should we bother to get the young Hawks? Let us kill this Turtle. He will make a fine breakfast for all of us. We must be careful or he will bite us. Let us throw a net over him and turn him over."

They had no nets with them, so they took some vines, and tore their clothes into strings and made a net.

But when they had put the net all over the Turtle, they could not roll him over. Instead, the Turtle suddenly dived down into the deep water. The men were so eager to get him that they did not let go of the net, so down they went into the water. As they came out they said: "Half the night a Kingfisher kept putting out our fires. Now we have torn

our clothes and got all wet trying to get this Turtle. We will build another fire, and at sunrise we will eat those young Hawks." And they began to build another fire.

The Mother Hawk heard them, and said to her mate: "Sooner or later these men will get our young. Do go and tell our friend the Lion."

At once the Father Hawk flew to the Lion.

"Why do you come at this hour of the night?" asked the Lion.

The Hawk told him the whole story.

The Lion said: "I will come at once. You go back and comfort your mate and the young ones." Soon the Lion came roaring.

When the hunters heard the Lion's roar they cried, "Now we shall all be killed." And away they ran as fast as they could go.

When the Lion came to the foot of the tree, not one of the hunters was to be seen. Then the Kingfisher and the Turtle came up, and the Hawks said: "You have saved us. Friends in need are friends indeed."

XIV

THE BRAVE LITTLE BOWMAN

ONCE upon a time there was a little man with a crooked back who was called the wise little bowman because he used his bow and arrow so very well. This crooked little man said to himself: "If I go to the king and ask him to let me join his army, he 's sure to ask what a little man like me is good for. I must find some great big man who will take me as his page, and ask the king to take us." So the little bowman went about the city looking for a big man.

One day he saw a big, strong man digging a ditch "What makes a fine big man like you do such work?" asked the little man.

"I do this work because I can earn a living in no other way," said the big man.

"Dig no more," said the bowman. "There is in this whole country no such bowman as I am; but no king would let me join his army because I am such a little man. I want you to ask the king to let you join the army. He will take you because you are big and strong. I will do the work that you are given to do, and we will divide the pay. In this way we shall both of us earn a good living. Will you come with me and do as I tell you?" asked the little bowman.

"Yes, I will go with you," said the big man.

So together they set out to go to the king. By and by they came to the gates of the palace, and sent word to the king that a wonderful bowman was there. The king sent for the bowman to come before him. Both the big man and the little man went in and, bowing, stood before the king.

The king looked at the big man and asked, "What brings you here?"

"I want to be in your army," said the big man.

"Who is the little man with you?" asked the king.

"He is my page," said the big man.

"What pay do you want?" asked the king.

"A thousand pieces a month for me and my page, O King," said the big man.

"I will take you and your page," said the king.

So the big man and the little bowman joined the king's army.

Now in those days there was a tiger in the forest who had carried off many people. The king sent for the big man and told him to kill that tiger.

The big man told the little bowman what the king said. They went into the forest together, and soon the little bowman shot the tiger.

The king was glad to be rid of the tiger, and gave the big man rich gifts and praised him.

Another day word came that a buffalo was running up and down a certain road. The king told the big man to go and kill that buffalo. The big man and the little man went to the road, and soon the little man shot the buffalo. When they both went back to the king, he gave a bag of money to the big man.

The king and all the people praised the big man, and so one day the big man said to the little man: "I can get on without you. Do you think there 's no bowman but yourself?" Many other harsh and unkind things did he say to the little man.

But a few days later a king from a far country marched upon the city and sent a message to its king saying, "Give up your country, or do battle."

The king at once sent his army. The big man was armed and mounted on a war-elephant. But the little bowman knew that the big man could not shoot, so he took his bow and seated himself behind the big man.

Then the war-elephant, at the head of the army, went out of the city. At the first beat of the drums, the big man

shook with fear. "Hold on tight," said the little bowman. "If you fall off now, you will be killed. You need not be afraid; I am here."

But the big man was so afraid that he slipped down off

the war-elephant's back, and ran back into the city. He did not stop until he reached his home.

"And now to win!" said the little bowman, as he drove the war-elephant into the fight. The army broke into the camp of the king that came from afar, and drove him back to his own country. Then the little bowman led the army back into the city. The king and all the people called him "the brave little bowman." The king made him the chief of the army, giving him rich gifts.

XV

THE FOOLHARDY WOLF

A LION bounded forth from his lair one day, looking north, west, south, and east. He saw a Buffalo and went to kill him.

The Lion ate all of the Buffalo-meat he wanted, and then went down to the lake for a drink.

As the Lion turned to go toward his den for a nap, he came upon a hungry Wolf.

The Wolf had no chance to get away, so he threw himself at the Lion's feet.

"What do you want?" the Lion asked.

"O Lion, let me be your servant," said the Wolf.

"Very well," said the Lion, "serve me, and you shall have good food to eat."

So saying, the Lion went into his den for his nap.

When he woke up, the Lion said to the Wolf: "Each day you must go to the mountain top, and see whether there are any elephants, or ponies, or buffaloes about. If you see any, come to me and say: 'Great Lion, come forth in thy might. Food is in sight.' Then I will kill and eat, and give part of the meat to you."

So day after day the Wolf climbed to the mountain top, and seeing a pony, or a buffalo, or an elephant, he went back to the den, and falling at the Lion's feet he said: "Great Lion, come forth in thy might. Food is in sight."

Then the Lion would bound forth and kill whichever beast it was, sharing the meat with the Wolf.

Now this Wolf had never had such fine meat to eat, nor so much. So as time went on, the Wolf grew bigger and bigger, and stronger and stronger, until he was really proud of his great size and strength.

"See how big and strong I am," he said to himself.

"Why am I living day after day on food given me by another? I will kill for my own eating. I 'll kill an elephant for myself."

So the Wolf went to the Lion, and said: "I want to eat an elephant of my own killing. Will you let me lie in your corner in the den, while you climb the mountain to look out for an elephant? Then when you see one, you come to the den and say, 'Great Wolf, come forth in thy might. Food is in sight.' Then I will kill the elephant."

Said the Lion: "Wolf, only Lions can kill elephants. The world has never seen a Wolf that could kill an elephant. Give up this notion of yours, and eat what I kill."

But no matter what the Lion said, the Wolf would not give way. So at last the Lion said: "Well, have your own way. Lie down in the den, and I will climb to the top of the mountain."

When he saw an elephant the Lion went back to the mouth of the cave, and said: "Great Wolf, come forth in thy might. Food is in sight."

Then from the den the Wolf nimbly bounded forth, ran to where the elephant was, and, howling three times, he sprang at the elephant.

But the Wolf missed his aim, and fell down at the ele-

phant's feet. The elephant raised his right foot and killed the Wolf.

Seeing all this, the Lion said, "You will no more come forth in your might, you foolhardy Wolf."

XVI

THE STOLEN PLOW

AT one time there were two traders who were great friends. One of them lived in a small village, and one lived in a large town near-by.

One day the village trader took his plow to the large town to have it mended. Then he left it with the trader who lived there. After some time the town trader sold the plow, and kept the money.

When the trader from the village came to get his plow the town trader said, "The mice have eaten your plow."

"That is strange! How could mice eat such a thing?" said the village trader.

That afternoon when all the children went down to the river to go swimming, the village trader took the town trader's little son to the house of a friend saying, "Please keep this little boy here until I come back for him."

By and by the villager went back to the town trader's house.

"Where is my son? He went away with you. Why did n't you bring him back?" asked the town trader.

"I took him with me and left him on the bank of the river while I went down into the water," said the villager. "While I was swimming about a big bird seized your son, and flew up into the air with him. I shouted, but I could not make the bird let go," he said.

"That cannot be true," cried the town trader. "No bird could carry off a boy. I will go to the court, and you will have to go there, and tell the judge."

The villager said, "As you please"; and they both went to the court. The town trader said to the judge:

"This fellow took my son with him to the river, and when I asked where the boy was, he said that a bird had carried him off."

"What have you to say?" said the judge to the village trader.

"I told the father that I took the boy with me, and that a bird had carried him off," said the village trader.

"But where in the world are there birds strong enough to carry off boys?" said the judge.

"I have a question to ask you," answered the village trader. "If birds cannot carry off boys, can mice eat plows?"

"What do you mean by that?" asked the judge.

"I left my good plow with this man. When I came for

it he told me that the mice had eaten it. If mice eat plows, then birds carry off boys; but if mice cannot do this, neither can birds carry off boys. This man says the mice ate my plow."

The judge said to the town trader, "Give back the plow to this man, and he will give your son back to you."

And the two traders went out of the court, and by nighttime one had his son back again, and the other had his plow.

XVII

THE LION IN BAD COMPANY

ONE day a young Lion came suddenly upon a Wolf. The Wolf was not able to get away, so he said to the Lion: "Please, Great Lion, could you take me to your den, and let me live with you and your mate? I will work for you all my days."

This young Lion had been told by his father and mother not to make friends with any Wolf. But when this Wolf called him "Great Lion," he said to himself: "This Wolf is not bad. This Wolf is not like other Wolves." So he took the Wolf to the den where he lived with his father and mother.

Now this Lion's father was a fine old Lion, and he told his son that he did not like having this Wolf there. But the young Lion thought he knew better than his father, so the Wolf stayed in the den.

One day the Wolf wanted horse-flesh to eat, so he said to the young Lion, "Sir, there is nothing we have not eaten except horse-meat; let us take a horse."

"But where are there horses?" asked the Lion.

"There are small ponies on the river bank," said the Wolf.

So the young Lion went with the Wolf to the river bank when the ponies were bathing. The Lion caught a small pony, and throwing it on his back, he ran back to his den.

His father said: "My son, those ponies belong to the king. Kings have many skilful archers. Lions do not live long who eat ponies belonging to the king. Do not take another pony."

But the young Lion liked the taste of horse-meat, and he caught and killed pony after pony.

Soon the king heard that a Lion was killing the ponies when they went to bathe in the river. "Build a tank inside the town," said the king. "The lion will not get the ponies there." But the Lion killed the ponies as they bathed in the tank.

Then the king said the ponies must be kept in the stables. But the Lion went over the wall, and killed the ponies in their stables.

At last the king called an archer, who shot like lightning. "Do you think you can shoot this Lion?" the king asked him. The archer said that he was sure he could. "Very well," said the king, "take your place in the tower on the wall, and shoot him." So the archer waited there in the tower.

By and by the Lion and the Wolf came to the wall. The Wolf did not go over the wall but waited to see what would happen. The Lion sprang over the wall. Very soon he caught and killed a pony. Then the archer let fly an arrow.

The Lion roared, "I am shot."

Then the Wolf said to himself: "The Lion has been shot, and soon he will die. I will now go back to my old home in the woods." And so he did.

The Lion fell down dead.

XVIII

THE WISE GOAT AND THE WOLF

ONCE upon a time, many, many wild Goats lived in a cave in the side of a hill. A Wolf lived with his mate not far from this cave. Like all Wolves they liked the taste of Goat-meat. So they caught the Goats, one after another, and ate them all but one who was wiser than all the others. Try as they might, the Wolves could not catch her.

One day the Wolf said to his mate: "My dear, let us play a trick on that wise Goat. I will lie down here pretending to be dead. You go alone to the cave where the Goat lives, and looking very sad, say to her: 'My dear, do you see my mate lying there dead? I am so sad; I have no friends. Will you be good to me? Will you come and help me bury the body of my mate?' The Goat will be sorry for you and I think she will come here with you. When she stands beside me I will spring upon her and bite her in the neck.

Then she will fall over dead, and we shall have good meat to eat."

The Wolf then lay down, and his mate went to the Goat, saying what she had been told to say.

But the wise Goat said: "My dear, all my family and friends have been eaten by your mate. I am afraid to go one step with you. I am far safer here than I would be there."

"Do not be afraid," said the Wolf. "What harm can a dead Wolf do to you?"

These and many more words the Wolf said to the Goat, so that at last the Goat said she would go with the Wolf.

But as they went up the hill side by side, the Goat said to herself: "Who knows what will happen? How do I know the Wolf is dead?" She said to the Wolf, "I think it will be better if you go on in front of me."

The Wolf thought he heard them coming. He was hungry and he raised up his head to see if he could see them. The Goat saw him raise his head, and she turned and ran back to her cave.

"Why did you raise your head when you were pretending to be dead?" the Wolf asked her mate. He had no good answer.

By and by the Wolves were both so very hungry that the

Wolf asked his mate to try once more to catch the Goat.

This time the Wolf went to the Goat and said: "My friend, your coming helped us, for as soon as you came, my

mate felt better. He is now very much better. Come and talk to him. Let us be friends and have a good time together."

THE WISE GOAT AND THE WOLF

The wise Goat thought: "These wicked Wolves want to play another trick on me. But I have thought of a trick to play on them." So the Goat said: "I will go to see your mate, and I will take my friends with me. You go back and get ready for us. Let us all have a good time together."

Then the Wolf was afraid, and she asked: "Who are the friends who will come with you? Tell me their names."

The wise Goat said: "I will bring the two Hounds, Old Gray and Young Tan, and that fine big dog called Four-Eyes. And I will ask each of them to bring his mate."

The Wolf waited to hear no more. She turned, and away she ran back to her mate. The Goat never saw either of them again.

XIX

PRINCE WICKED AND THE GRATEFUL ANIMALS

ONCE upon a time a king had a son named Prince Wicked. He was fierce and cruel, and he spoke to nobody without abuse, or blows. Like grit in the eye, was Prince Wicked to every one, both in the palace and out of it.

His people said to one another, "If he acts this way while he is a prince, how will he act when he is king?"

One day when the prince was swimming in the river, suddenly a great storm came on, and it grew very dark.

In the darkness the servants who were with the prince swam from him, saying to themselves, "Let us leave him alone in the river, and he may drown."

When they reached the shore, some of the servants who had not gone into the river said, "Where is Prince Wicked?"

"Is n't he here?" they asked. "Perhaps he came out of the river in the darkness and went home." Then the servants all went back to the palace.

The king asked where his son was, and again the servants said: "Is n't he here, O King? A great storm came on soon after we went into the water. It grew very dark. When we came out of the water the prince was not with us."

At once the king had the gates thrown open. He and all his men searched up and down the banks of the river for the missing prince. But no trace of him could be found.

In the darkness the prince had been swept down the river. He was crying for fear he would drown when he came across a log. He climbed upon the log, and floated farther down the river.

When the great storm arose, the water rushed into the homes of a Rat and a Snake who lived on the river bank. The Rat and the Snake swam out into the river and found the same log the prince had found. The Snake climbed upon one end of the log, and the Rat climbed upon the other.

On the river's bank a cottonwood-tree grew, and a young Parrot lived in its branches. The storm pulled up this tree, and it fell into the river. The heavy rain beat down the Parrot when it tried to fly, and it could not go far. Looking down it saw the log and flew down to rest. Now there were four on the log floating down stream together.

Just around the bend in the river a certain poor man had built himself a hut. As he walked to and fro late at night listening to the storm, he heard the loud cries of the prince. The poor man said to himself: "I must get that man out of the water. I must save his life." So he shouted: "I will save you! I will save you!" as he swam out in the river.

Soon he reached the log, and pushing it by one end, he

soon pushed it into the bank. The prince jumped up and down, he was so glad to be safe and sound on dry land.

Then the poor man saw the Snake, the Rat, and the Parrot, and carried them to his hut. He built a fire, putting the animals near it so they could get dry. He took care of them first, because they were the weaker, and afterwards he looked after the comfort of the prince.

Then the poor man brought food and set it before them, looking after the animals first and the prince afterwards. This made the young prince angry, and he said to himself: "This poor man does not treat me like a prince. He takes

care of the animals before taking care of me." Then the prince began to hate the poor man.

A few days later, when the prince, and the Snake, the Rat, and the Parrot were rested, and the storm was all over, the Snake said good-by to the poor man with these words:

"Father, you have been very kind to me. I know where there is some buried gold. If ever you want gold, you have only to come to my home and call, 'Snake!' and I will show you the buried gold. It shall all be yours."

Next the Rat said good-by to the poor man. "If ever you want money," said the Rat, "come to my home, and call out, 'Rat!' and I will show you where a great deal of money is buried near my home. It shall all be yours."

Then the Parrot came, saying: "Father, silver and gold have I none, but if you ever want choice rice, come to where I live and call, 'Parrot!' and I will call all my family and friends together, and we will gather the choicest rice in the fields for you."

Last came the prince. In his heart he hated the poor man who had saved his life. But he pretended to be as thankful as the animals had been, saying, "Come to me when I am king, and I will give you great riches." So saying, he went away.

Not long after this the prince's father died, and Prince Wicked was made king. He was then very rich.

By and by the poor man said to himself: "Each of the four whose lives I saved made a promise to me. I will see if they will keep their promises."

First of all he went to the Snake, and standing near his hole, the poor man called out, "Snake!"

At once the Snake darted forth, and with every mark of respect he said: "Father, in this place there is much gold. Dig it up and take it all."

"Very well," said the poor man. "When I need it, I will not forget."

After visiting for a while, the poor man said good-by to the Snake, and went to where the Rat lived, calling out, "Rat!"

The Rat came at once, and did as the Snake had done, showing the poor man where the money was buried.

"When I need it, I will come for it," said the poor man.

Going next to the Parrot, he called out, "Parrot!" and the bird flew down from the tree-top as soon as he heard the call.

"O Father," said the Parrot, "shall I call together all my family and friends to gather choice rice for you?"

The poor man, seeing that the Parrot was willing and ready to keep his promise, said: "I do not need rice now. If ever I do, I will not forget your offer."

Last of all, the poor man went into the city where the king lived. The king, seated on his great white elephant, was riding through the city. The king saw the poor man, and said to himself: "That poor man has come to ask me for the great riches I promised to give him. I must have his head cut off before he can tell the people how he saved my life when I was the prince."

So the king called his servants to him and said: "You see that poor man over there? Seize him and bind him, beat him at every corner of the street as you march him out of the city, and then chop off his head."

The servants had to obey their king. So they seized and bound the poor man. They beat him at every corner of the street. The poor man did not cry out, but he said, over and over again, "It is better to save poor, weak animals than to save a prince."

At last some wise men among the crowds along the street asked the poor man what prince he had saved. Then the poor man told the whole story, ending with the words, "By saving your king, I brought all this pain upon myself."

The wise men and all the rest of the crowd cried out: "This poor man saved the life of our king, and now the king has ordered him to be killed. How can we be sure that he will not have any, or all, of us killed? Let us kill him." And in their anger they rushed from every side upon the king as he rode on his elephant, and with arrows and stones they killed him then and there.

Then they made the poor man king, and set him to rule over them.

The poor man ruled his people well. One day he decided once more to try the Snake, the Rat, and the Parrot. So, followed by many servants, the king went to where the Snake lived.

At the call of "Snake!" out came the Snake from his hole, saying, "Here, O King, is your treasure; take it."

"I will," said the king. "And I want you to come with me."

Then the king had his servants dig up the gold.

Going to where the Rat lived, the king called, "Rat!" Out came the Rat, and bowing low to the king, the Rat said, "Take all the money buried here and have your servants carry it away."

"I will," said the king, and he asked the Rat to go with him and the Snake.

Then the king went to where the Parrot lived, and called, "Parrot!" The Parrot flew down to the king's feet and said, "O King, shall I and my family and my friends gather choice rice for you?"

"Not now, not until rice is needed," said the king. "Will you come with us?" The Parrot was glad to join them.

So with the gold, and the money, and with the Snake, the Rat, and the Parrot as well, the king went back to the city.

The king had the gold and the money hidden away in the palace. He had a tube of gold made for the Snake to live in. He had a glass box made for the Rat's home, and a cage of gold for the Parrot. Each had the food he liked best of all to eat every day, and so these four lived happily all their lives.

XX

BEAUTY AND BROWNIE

TWO Deer named Beauty and Brownie lived with their father and mother and great herds of Deer in a forest. One day their father called them to him and said: "The Deer in the forest are always in danger when the corn is ripening in the fields. It will be best for you to go away for a while, and you must each take your own herd of Deer with you."

"What is the danger, Father?" they asked.

"When the Deer go into the fields to eat the corn they get caught in the traps the men set there," the father said. "Many Deer are caught in these traps every year."

"Shall you go away with us?" Brownie said.

"No, your mother and I, and some of the other old Deer will stay here in the forest," said the father. "There will be food enough for us, but there is not enough for you and your herds. You must lead your herds up into the high hills where there is plenty of food for you, and stay there

until the crops are all cut. Then you can bring your herds back here. But you must be careful.

"You must travel by night, because the hunters will see you if you go by day. And you must not take your herd near the villages where hunters live."

So Beauty and Brownie and their herds set out. Beauty traveled at night and did not go near any villages, and at last brought his herd safely to the high hills. Not a single Deer did Beauty lose.

But Brownie forgot what his father had said. Early each morning he started off with his herd, going along all through the day. When he saw a village, he led his herd right past it. Again and again hunters saw the herd, and they killed many, many of the Deer in Brownie's herd.

When crops had been cut, the Deer started back to the forest. Beauty led all his herd back, but stupid Brownie traveled in the daytime, and again he took his herd past the villages. When he reached the forest only a few were left of all Brownie's herd.

XXI

THE ELEPHANT AND THE DOG

ONCE upon a time a Dog used to go into the stable where the king's Elephant lived. At first the Dog went there to get the food that was left after the Elephant had finished eating.

Day after day the Dog went to the stable, waiting around for bits to eat. But by and by the Elephant and the Dog came to be great friends. Then the Elephant began to share his food with the Dog, and they ate together. When the Elephant slept, his friend the Dog slept beside him. When the Elephant felt like playing, he would catch the Dog in his trunk and swing him to and fro. Neither the Dog nor the Elephant was quite happy unless the other was near-by.

One day a farmer saw the Dog and said to the Elephant-keeper: "I will buy that Dog. He looks good-tempered, and I see that he is smart. How much do you want for the Dog?"

The Elephant-keeper did not care for the Dog, and he did want some money just then. So he asked a fair price, and the farmer paid it and took the Dog away to the country.

The king's Elephant missed the Dog and did not care to eat when his friend was not there to share the food. When the time came for the Elephant to bathe, he would not bathe. The next day again the Elephant would not eat, and he would not bathe. The third day, when the Elephant would neither eat nor bathe, the king was told about it.

The king sent for his chief servant, saying, "Go to the stable and find out why the Elephant is acting in this way."

The chief servant went to the stable and looked the Elephant all over. Then he said to the Elephant-keeper: "There seems to be nothing the matter with this Elephant's body, but why does he look so sad? Has he lost a playmate?"

"Yes," said the keeper, "there was a Dog who ate and

slept and played with the Elephant. The Dog went away three days ago."

"Do you know where the Dog is now?" asked the chief servant.

"No, I do not," said the keeper.

Then the chief servant went back to the king and said,

"The Elephant is not sick, but he is lonely without his friend, the Dog."

"Where is the Dog?" asked the king.

"A farmer took him away, so the Elephant-keeper says," said the chief servant. "No one knows where the farmer lives."

"Very well," said the king. "I will send word all over the country, asking the man who bought this Dog to turn him loose. I will give him back as much as he paid for the Dog."

When the farmer who had bought the Dog heard this, he turned him loose. The Dog ran back as fast as ever he could go to the Elephant's stable. The Elephant was so glad to see the Dog that he picked him up with his trunk and put him on his head. Then he put him down again.

When the Elephant-keeper brought food, the Elephant watched the Dog as he ate, and then took his own food.

All the rest of their lives the Elephant and the Dog lived together.